Gemma's Angel

The Girl from Chiapas
A Tale of Loss, Love and Redemption

R. Annan

Gemma's Angel

Copyright 2009 by R. Annan
WGA Reg. #: R26489 (08/19/2009)

Author's Portrait by Hazel Tertsakian
Copy Editor: Karren Doll Tolliver
Photography © L. Annan

One Vision Publishing
Published 2017
ISBN: 978-1-942338-09-3 (eBook)
ISBN: 978-1-942338-08-6 (Print)

Other books by R. Annan: *Mr. Dobbs: A Christmas Ghost Story*; *The Ghost of Reginald Burton, Esquire*; *Vzor's Prisoner: A Sci-fi Novel*; *The Princess of Ovaar: A Sci-fi Fantasy*; *Sen Loi*; *The Barnhart Intruder*.

Western novels by R. Annan include: *The Fight for the Lazy M*; *The Red Bandana*; *The Salvation of Truce Logan*; *The Cowboy from Sierra Blanca*; *Jack Cordell Westerns*; *Clay Jared Westerns*; *Jesse Garnett Westerns*.

Chapter 1

"No evil shall befall thee, neither shall any plague come nigh to thee. For he shall give his Angels charge over thee to keep thee in all his ways." Psalms 91:10-11

* * *

On a clear, sunny afternoon in 1959 a young Hispanic girl, dressed like a farm worker, followed a path outside Reynosa. The path led her through a stand of scrub oaks to a grassy slope that ran down to the south bank of the Rio Grande River. Having traveled for many days, she was very tired.

After looking around, the girl moved off the path and sat down with her canvas bag. Using it for a pillow, she laid back on the grass, looked up at the clear blue sky and started to think about past events.

"How did you come to this place?" she asked herself. *"What are you doing here, so far away from your little farm in Chiapas?"*

The answer came quickly in a flood of painful memories.

It all began in Chiapas at the sharecropping farm where she and her husband lived and worked. The landlord not only owned the farm but he also owned the farm store where the farmers were expected to buy whatever it offered, which was often very little. To make things worse, the landlord continually raised the price of canned goods, seeds and other things, regardless of the hardship it caused the workers. They had little money to spare and prices were already so high they could barely afford to pay for the necessities of life.

But no one dared to complain for fear of losing their little patch of land. Each day, each week, each month they fell further and further in debt to the landlord. Then one day, a group of them gathered together to discuss the matter and decide on a course of action.

After much drinking and brave talk, they decided to go over to the landlord's house and ask him to be reasonable and lower some of the prices. If he was a good man, he would listen. After all, he went to the same church as they did and worshiped the same God as they did. At least they had that much in common with the landlord. Maybe that would count for something.

As they walked the five miles along the road to the landlord's house, many of them drank tequila, sang songs and shouted. They were feeling very optimistic and their spirits were high.

But when they got there, the landlord refused to come outside and talk to them. Emboldened with drink, they pounded on the big iron gate in front of his house and chanted loud slogans. When the landlord heard the racket, he called up his guards and they ran to the gate with fixed bayonets and loaded rifles.

As did many of the women that day, the girl had decided to go along with her man even though she was late with child. Her husband had argued and pleaded with her to stay home, but she was stubborn and refused. She had a feeling that something bad was going to happen. Before setting out she lit a candle and prayed that nothing would go wrong.

But that day nothing went right and everything went wrong. One of the farmers who was very drunk fired his old, rusty pistol into the air. It made a roaring bang as it exploded in his face, killing him instantly and wounding one of the landlord's men.

Reacting quickly, the landlord's guards fired their weapons point blank into the farmers, killing some and wounding others. The poor farmers and their wives began howling and screaming. There was instant chaos as they scattered and ran, knocking each other down as they tried to escape the bullets.

The girl was thrown to the ground. Confused and dazed, she got on her hands and knees and looked around for her husband. Several times she screamed out his name, "Raoul! Raoul!"

Tears streamed down her face and fear blazed in her eyes as she continued to shout his name again and again. At last she saw where he lay badly wounded on the blood soaked earth. When she crawled to his side and tried to lift him, something tore in her stomach. She groaned in pain and fell back on the ground, almost fainting.

Several times again she tried to lift him, but his weight was too much for her. With a heart rending moan, she finally gave up and scrambled away on hands and knees, cursing herself for being such a coward for leaving him there. But she had to go because the baby was pushing on her stomach. Her only thought then was for the baby.

"God forgive me!" she cried as she struggled to her feet.

Hobbling along, she held her stomach trying to keep up the others. The sound of gunfire followed them. It was almost nightfall. She fell several times, got up, and went on again. Pain brought a flood of tears to her eyes and blinded her so that she could hardly see where she was going.

Tripping over a rock, she fell into a ravine, landed on her stomach and slid down a long slope, skinning her arms and legs.

"I'm going to die," she thought. And then, mercifully, she fainted.

When she regained her senses, the girl realized she was not dead but was in a little tin shack near a stream by the side of a road. The shack belonged to an old lady who sold boiled corn she stole from the landlord's cornfields at night.

She found the girl in the ravine behind her shack and dragged her inside to take care of her. As for the baby, it was stillborn and had to be taken. The old lady made a little grave for it in the woods behind the shack. For many days, the girl cried and mourned the loss of her husband and child.

Eventually she became strong enough to help the old lady with selling the corn. They boiled it in a big tin drum alongside the road. Truck drivers stopped at all hours to buy it and chat with the girl. Many gave her extra money for a quick kiss. She saved this on the side.

From the truck drivers, the girl learned the authorities were still looking for anyone who had taken part in what they called a rebellion. Of course, there had been no rebellion but it didn't matter to the landlord because he had the power to take the lands of everyone involved. Many of the farmers were arrested and put in prison, and others just disappeared.

One day the girl told the old lady, "I must go. If they find me here, it will be bad for you. I wouldn't want that to happen."

The old lady looked sad because she liked the girl very much. She sighed, went into the shack and came out with something in her hand. She gave it to the girl and the girl studied it for a while, puzzled by its shape. It had a sinister look about it and was heavy and made of shiny steel.

"What is it?" the girl asked.

"What do you think it is?" the old lady said.

"It looks like a barrette, for the hair," the girl said.

"Yes, but a special one. In the old days, when I was young, we wore these in our hair to protect us from being attacked by passionate men who were possessed by lustful demons."

The old lady held the barrette in her hand like a weapon. It had five prongs, like on a fork, each about two inches long that came to a sharp point. Above them was a slot long enough to slip the fingers through. It fit her hand nicely and was easy to hold.

"It looks like a cat's claw," the girl said. The old lady made a slashing motion in the air with her hand. The girl's eyes widened. She nodded that she understood.

"Yes. That is why we call it the, *garra del gata*," the old one said. "The claw of the cat."

The old lady motioned to the girl to turn around. She rearranged her long hair into a bun behind her neck and fastened it in place with the barrette. "Can you do it like this, by yourself?"

"Yes," the girl said. "I have done it with a barrette many times, as a child."

"Good. If you need it, just reach back and pull it out. When you go to bed, always keep it near."

"Thank you," the girl said. "But I must pay you for it."

"No. You have thanked me and that is enough. I don't need it anymore, but perhaps you will."

In a few days, the girl left. It was a sad goodbye.

Chapter 2

After leaving the old lady, the girl traveled west for many months and then northeast, going from one farm to another picking vegetables and fruits. When that got tiresome, she found work at a small *pensiones* where tourists came from America and Canada. The owners didn't pay her much, but gave her food and a place to sleep. It was easier and cleaner than working in the fields.

The visitors from the north often left books, American newspapers, and magazines as well as Spanish-American dictionaries. Whenever possible, the girl kept them. She took an interest in learning English and taught herself many of the common phrases, using them whenever she had a chance.

Two years went by as the girl slowly worked her way northeast across the country. One day she heard talk about a border town called Reynosa. It was a place where they took farm workers across the Rio Grande River into Texas. A person could make more money in Texas in a month than in Mexico for a year.

The best part was, you could go back and forth, as you wished. People talked about what a good deal it was across the river. She thought it over, decided to give it a try and headed for Reynosa. At Reynosa, they told her where to meet the guide down by the Rio Grande. There was a trail east of town. He would come along about noon that day.

And now here she sat looking across the river at a place that promised a new and uncertain future, but only if she had the courage to grab it.

Her thoughts were broken by the sound of voices. A big man came down the path with six people following him. The girl jumped up, grabbed her canvas bag and ran to join them. When the leader saw her, he stopped everyone at the edge of the river and waited.

As she approached him, he looked her over. "You have to pay me," he said with authority. He was a heavy man with a beard and smelled of beer, garlic, and sweat.

"How much?" the girl asked.

"Three hundred, American," the leader replied.

In Reynosa, where she exchanged her *pesos* for dollars, they told her the going price was two hundred, American. They said that the man worked for a big farm in Texas, and she was guaranteed a high paying job picking melons and other vegetables. He took workers across the river to a pickup area where a truck from the farm would come and get them. The man would then return across the river to Reynosa and wait for more customers. He made a good living that way.

"I only have two hundred, American," the girl said.

"For you, alright," the leader said, grinning broadly. His teeth were yellowish brown from cigarette smoke.

The girl didn't like the way this man stared at her. It was indecent. She thought about changing her mind, but decided to go on. After all, she had come too far to turn back now.

The girl gave the leader the money and they started walking again. He found a shallow place that made it easy to cross the river. The girl stopped for a moment to look back. Suddenly, she felt alone and sad. Leaving her country for a new one, was not an easy thing to do. There was no knowing if she would ever come back again. For a moment, she had doubts and felt afraid.

A rough voice interrupted her thoughts. "Hey, girl! You coming or not?" the leader yelled at her. She hurried to catch up.

They walked at a slow pace, stopping several times to rest. She hadn't brought any water but an old man was kind enough to share his canteen with her. She learned he was also from Chiapas, and they talked as they walked along. She noticed the leader kept staring at her and it made her feel dirty. After a while he stopped everyone. He spoke to another man in the group.

"Take them up to the big clearing and stay there until the truck comes. I have some business to attend to," the leader told the man.

The man shrugged and led the group away. As they moved out, the leader grabbed the girl by her arm and pulled her aside.

"What are you doing?" she asked.

For an answer, he shoved her into a nearby stand of scrub oaks, out of sight of the others.

"What do you want from me?" she asked.

"Shut up and lay down!" he growled through nicotine stained teeth.

"No, I lay down for no one," the girl said.

"You will lay down for me," he growled.

The leader hit her so hard in the stomach she lost her breath and gasped for air. He pushed her hard and she fell back onto the ground. As soon as she was down he knelt over her and took out a knife.

"If you scream I will cut you," he said.

"I will not scream," she replied through clenched teeth, leering up at him. She reached back behind her head and felt for the cat's claw.

"What are you doing?" he asked.

"Letting my hair down," she said

"Why are you letting your hair down, girl?"

"So you can kiss the claw of the cat!"

Her hand moved in a blur and the leader felt something hit his neck. At first, he thought it was a bee. Seconds later, a white tunnel opened and closed in his mind. His world faded to black.

Up ahead, the group came to the designated clearing just as a truck with a canvass covered cargo space pulled up. Two American men got out of the cab. One was tall and thin, and the other was short and chubby.

"Where's Jose?" the tall American asked.

"He's back there with a girl." The old man from Chiapas told him.

"Do you think she's worth waiting for?" the short American asked the old man.

"Yes," the old man said.

"Are you sure?" the tall American asked.

"Yes, I am sure," the old man answered. "She is from Chiapas. Girls from Chiapas are good workers."

The two Americans laughed.

"Maybe she won't be so good anymore, when Jose is finished with her," the short American chuckled. "I hear Jose is quite a lover boy."

"Yeah, well maybe one of these days he'll bite off more than he can chew," the tall American replied. He paused a moment and looked down the path. "We can't wait. It'll be dark soon. Let's load up."

They loaded everyone onto the truck and were about to leave when the girl from Chiapas came running into view. She jumped up into the truck with the others. As they drove away, she rearranged her hair into a bun and put the barrette back in place. The old man saw the barrette and smiled. He knew what it was and what it was used for.

A man in the group chuckled and said to the girl, "That Jose, he's really something, isn't he?"

"No," the girl said flatly. "He is nothing."

The man started to reply, but stopped as the old man from Chiapas tapped him on the arm. "Forget about Jose," he said. "He has gone back across the river. His work is done here."

The man looked confused for a moment. "Oh," he said and moved further away from the girl.

The truck gained speed, leaving a cloud of ocher colored dust behind. The girl, stared back down the path. She couldn't see the river now, but knew it was there, a line between the known and the unknown, between the past and the future. After a while there was only the dust shutting out the sunlight.

The girl from Chiapas made the sign of the cross. The old man saw her and did the same. The others did also.

Chapter 3

Frail, silver haired widow Gemma Duvalier was a loner. She lived in a white, two story wooden house on 21 Pine Street, in the small town of Hudson, in west central Florida. It was a well maintained house, with a neatly trimmed front lawn. A high, wooden fence ran along the sides and around the back, providing privacy for the swimming pool.

Located near the Gulf of Mexico, Hudson was a quiet town. Often, when a cool front from the east met a warm front from the Gulf, a dense fog would develop. It gave the town a spooky, almost deserted look. After hanging on all night, the fog would reluctantly melt away as the sun came up in the morning.

Most of the people who lived on Pine Street were elderly and retired just like Gemma. They also hired people to keep everything working and looking nice and neat. Time on Pine Street passed smooth and orderly. The garbage was collected on certain designated days and the mail came every afternoon on schedule.

For the most part, everyone on Pine Street kept pretty much to themselves. You hardly ever saw anyone except when they came out of their homes to collect the mail or go to the store. A stranger driving down Pine Street couldn't help but think the people in those nice, clean white houses led happy, secure and contented lives.

For the most part, that was true for Gemma Duvalier. She led a simple life. Her contact with the outside world was mostly through the newspaper, her vintage radio, and an old, black dial phone that she kept on the stand along with the oil paints and brushes.

Next to the stand, facing the window, was an artist's easel. On the easel was an unfinished painting of a desert scene that Gemma worked on whenever she felt the urge. She was in no hurry to finish it.

Gemma usually didn't leave her house, except on occasion. Most of her days were spent in the bright, sunny lanai, with its wide, louvered windows, and screen door. It was conveniently located off the kitchen, facing the back yard and pool. Gemma often ate at a card table there.

In one far corner was a comfortable chaise lounge with an end table and lamp. The chaise was where she read until late into the night. She preferred that to sleeping upstairs in her big, lonely bedroom. Sleep came hard up there and when it did she usually had bad dreams.

The lanai was Gemma's oasis. It was light, cool, airy, and very friendly.

The one bright spot in Gemma's life was Gino, the pool boy. This handsome, muscular, suntanned adonis dressed in his tight, faded jeans and tight, sheer T-shirt, came every Friday to clean the pool. On the last Friday of the month, after finishing up, he would come into the lanai to collect his twenty dollars and they would talk.

One Friday Gino knocked on the lanai door and Gemma invited him in as usual.

"Good afternoon, Mrs. Duvalier," Gino said very politely. "Sorry to bother you ma'am. I just finished the pool." The subtext here was that he wanted his money.

"How does it look, Gino?" Gemma asked.

"Oh, fine ma'am. The chlorine and pH levels are perfect," Gino said. "I had to replace the filter, though."

"Oh? How much is that?"

"Ah, nineteen dollars, ma'am," Gino replied. "But it should be good for another six months. Maybe longer."

"That's good," Gemma said. Not wanting the conversation to die out, she quickly added, "How is business these days, Gino?"

"Oh, pretty good ma'am."

The conversation was about to end there when he suddenly told her about the place he goes to where the woman has five cats and one of the cats likes to swim in the pool. They both laughed about a cat swimming in a pool. Then he told her about his boat, an old sail boat with an outboard that he bought cheap and was fixing up.

"Would you like a cup of coffee, Gino? Or some chips, maybe?"

"Oh, no ma'am. I just had a burger over at the drive-in. Thanks anyway."

Gino stood there looking anxious to go, so Gemma walked over to the stand. She took some money out of the top drawer, came back and gave it to him. He put it in his wallet and went to the door and turned.

"See you next week, ma'am," Gino said, giving Gemma a warm smile.

"Yes. Goodbye, Gino," Gemma replied, as if she were bidding a sad farewell to a dear, dear friend.

Once Gino had left, Gemma stood all alone in the sunny, quiet, emptiness of the lanai. She sighed, went over to the chaise lounge and picked up a book that was on the end table next to it. Stretching out on the chaise, she began to read. After a while her head began to nod and she relaxed.

As Gemma dozed off, she let the book slide slowly to the floor. Outside, by the pool, a bird began a serenade but she didn't hear it.

Chapter 4

It was dark and the air was cooler now. In the moonlight, the road stretched east and west like a long, silver, serpentine ribbon. The girl walked slowly along with her head bent down, hugging herself to keep warm. Each step was an effort.

She had recently left a farm and was dressed in work clothes. Her hands were dry and sore and her legs and back ached after a long day of bending and lifting. Yet, even in men's worn clothes, it could be seen she was a woman.

From the corner of her eye, she caught the glow of headlights coming up fast behind her from the west. As it got closer, she saw it was an old pickup truck with high springs and a running board. It slowed down and the driver, who was a man, stared out at her as he passed by. She caught a glimpse of a gun rack in the rear window.

The truck finally came to a stop a good way down the road and the driver honked the horn several times to get her attention.

With her canvas bag slung over her shoulder, the girl started running. By the time she got to the truck, she was exhausted. The driver leaned towards the passenger side, pushed the door open and motioned for the girl to get in. She hesitated, staring into the cab.

"Well, in or out, girl?" the driver said in a raspy voice. "I ain't got all night."

She dropped her bag onto the floorboard, hoisted herself up onto the filthy, smelly seat and closed the door. The cab was warm and the smell of stale beer, cigarette smoke, and sweat was overpowering.

"Cold out there, ain't it?" the driver said. He had a weirdly hollow, nasal voice.

"Yes," the girl replied.

She stared ahead, not wanting to make eye contact. Eye contact was bad. It gave them crazy ideas. The man's odd sounding voice seemed strange to her.

"Been pickin' beans an' sech, have ya?" the man asked. It almost sounded as if he was talking through his nose.

"Yes, senor."

"Where ya headed?"

The girl shrugged. "Georgia. Maybe Florida."

"When'd you come across?" The man pulled something from his shirt pocket with one hand and put it between his lips. He pushed the cigarette lighter in.

"Last year."

"Where you from?"

"Chiapas."

"That's where they had the farmer's rebellion, ain't it?"

"I don't know," the girl replied. The man lit the thing in his mouth, inhaled deeply and exhaled a cloud of sweet smoke into the cab.

"You don't know?"

"No, I don't know."

"Sure you do. You know," the man said mockingly. "All you wetbacks know about that."

The girl suddenly knew she was in trouble. She turned her head to stare at the man. His bald head had a sort of skeletal look with eyes that blazed deep in their sockets. There was a slackness in his mouth, as if he had no teeth. His ears were too large for his head and a part of his nose seemed to be missing, perhaps from an accident of some sort. He made a wheezing sound when he breathed.

"You're real pretty for a spic," the man said.

The girl stiffened. This was always how it started. Suddenly he said, without warning, "How about doin' me?" He hadn't wasted any time.

She was prepared for it. "I can't, I'm sick," she said.

"I'm sick, too," he said, "so what's the difference? Come on."

"No," she insisted, "I better not." She paused a moment. "Maybe later, at a motel."

"Motel?" the man chuckled. "You must be dreaming. There ain't gonna be no motel."

"Well, I'm sorry, mister. I just can't."

"Okay, then, you're gonna end up like them two."

The girl was puzzled. "What two?"

"The two I got tied up in the back."

The girl turned and looked out through the space between the rifles on the gun rack in the rear window. Some of the light in the cab shined back there, onto the truck bed.

She could barely make out what looked like two women tied up and gagged.

She turned to leer across at the man and whimpered in a frightened voice, "Who are you, mister?"

The man chuckled. "Me? I'm the invisible man. I don't exist."

"Let me out, please!"

"If you do me, I'll make it quick," the man said, He ran a finger across his throat. "You won't feel a thing."

"Please, senor, let me out!"

Suddenly the man back handed the girl, knocking her head against the corner of the cab. She groaned in pain. Dazed, she put a finger to her lower lip. It came away warm and bloody. She shook her head to clear it.

"I'm only going to ask you once more," the man said. He pulled a knife from somewhere. The blade sparkled in the light of the dashboard. Holding the point against her left side, he growled, "One more time, yes or no?"

"No!"

The girl quickly reached her right hand back behind her neck to her hair, then quickly brought it forward in an arc. Metal flashed as she made a swift horizontal swipe, raking the barrette's prongs down the man's right eye, cheek and chin.

Howling loudly in pain, the man grabbed his face with both hands. The girl braced herself as the truck swerved off the road, rammed hard into a ditch and suddenly stalled. The man slumped silently over the steering wheel. The windshield was shattered where his head smashed into it. His neck was broken.

Reaching down to the dashboard, the girl turned the headlights off, jumped out onto the ground and rushed to the back of the truck. Hoisting herself up onto the truck bed, she untied the two women. One was middle aged and the other was young enough to be her daughter.

"Thank you," the old one said. "God bless you, sister."

"You better go before somebody comes," the girl replied.

"He took our money," the woman said. She disappeared into the darkness.

The girl looked at the young one. "Where were you going?"

"Back home to Coahuila," she answered, sobbing.

The older woman returned with a roll of money and the man's knife. She offered some of the money to the girl.

"No. I have plenty," the girl said. "You better go. If a car comes, hide in the bushes."

"My daughter and I thank you," the older woman said. The two of them got their bags from the back of the truck and walked fast down the road, heading west.

The girl got her own bag out of the truck cab, slung it over her shoulder and starting walking east on the road, clutching the barrette in her hand.

She glanced back once with fear in her eyes and started to run.

Chapter 5

It was well after midnight when a bus from Valdosta, on the way to Tampa, stopped behind a station in the small west central Florida town of Hudson. It was late September and a cold front from the north was mixing with warm air from the Gulf of Mexico. A dense blanket of fog crawled up every street and alley in town. It was hip high. As the bus stopped it swirled about the wheels like a serpent.

While the engine was still running, the door opened and a short man wearing a seedy suit got out. He looked around then pulled his hat low over his forehead, casting his eyes in shadow. From his looks, he appeared to be in his mid-forties. He had a paunchy yet muscular body.

The man walked straight through the bus station to the sidewalk out front. Once there, he took a switchblade knife from his pocket, leaned back against the station wall and began cleaning his fingernails.

The uniformed driver was next to step out of the bus. He was followed by a businessman in an expensive suit. The driver stretched and lit a cigarette. The businessman looked around.

"How far to Tampa?" the businessman asked, yawning.

"About sixty miles," the driver said.

"Where are we now?"

"Hudson."

The businessman noticed the fog. "Where's the fog coming from?"

"The Gulf. It's not far away."

The businessman sniffed the air, nodding. "I can smell the salt water."

"Yeah."

A girl carrying a canvas bag, with her hair up in a bun and dressed in men's work clothes, came sleepy eyed out of the bus. With her head down she walked past the driver and businessman and into the station.

"She's not very friendly," the businessman said. "I tried to talk to her. Quiet as a clam. Nice looking, though."

"She's one of them Mexican illegals. You see lots of them around here. Most of them don't speak much English," the driver replied. "Some of them are real friendly, if you know what I mean."

"Not her. I tried.

The driver took two more drags on his cigarette and flicked it tumbling into the fog. He looked at his watch and got back on the bus with the businessman following close behind. A few seconds later the door closed and the bus roared away. It was quickly swallowed up by the fog.

Out in front of the station, the man looked up and down the road. Five minutes later, the pool boy drove up in his battered truck and stopped. The man climbed in and Gino drove away.

"I don't like to be left waiting, kid." The man's voice was urban, deep and guttural, like someone who had a sore throat or smoked too much. His face was red and puffy from excess drinking.

"What? A few minutes? Come on Turner, don't be such an old grump," Gino said.

Turner's switch blade seemed to come out of nowhere. It flicked across Gino's line of sight, leaving a small nick on his right cheek.

"Hey!" Gino yelled, pulling away. "What the heck was that for?"

"For making me wait, kid," Turner said in that low, harsh, growling voice.

"Are you crazy? You cut me!"

"It's nothing. Stop crying like a baby."

They drove on in silence until Gino said, "How come you left Valdosta?"

"I had to hurt somebody in Valdosta, kid. Somebody who crossed me. Don't ever cross me."

Gino glanced at Turner. "So, you jumped bail in Valdosta, huh?"

"Yeah, so what?"

"They'll be looking for you, won't they?"

"They think I'm heading for Miami. I left that impression." Then, "Whatta you been up to, kid?"

"I've got my own little business."

"Doing what?"

"Cleaning pools."

"Cleaning pools, huh?" Turner said. He reflected on Gino's words for a moment, then added, "That could come in handy."

"Whatta you mean?"

"You go into people's homes sometimes, don't you?"

"Sure, so what?"

"Nothin'. We'll talk about it later," Turner replied. "Right now I'm hungry. Go find a burger joint."

They drove across town to a burger place. Only a few people were there at that late hour. Turner took a booth as Gino went for the food. He came back with burgers, fries, and coffee.

As they sat eating, Turner suddenly said, "Sometimes I like to burn places."

"Burn places?"

"Yeah. Burn places."

"What kind of places?"

"Any kind. Houses, stores, warehouses, anyplace."

"What for?"

"For the kick. I come back, stand in the crowd and watch the action. I look at the faces, listen to what people say. There's lots of screaming and crying. It's a lot of fun. You should try it."

"Me? No, I wouldn't do anything like that."

"Yeah, you always were a wimp."

"I'm cautious, is all."

Turner sneered. "No, you're a wimp, plain and simple, kid. And you'll die like that, afraid to take a chance."

"I'm thinking about something. It might pan out." Gino said defensively.

"Oh, really?" Turner sounded interested.

"Yeah. It might pan out. You want a piece of the action?"

As soon as the words came out Gino was sorry he said them. It was a lie he had made up on the spur of the moment, just to impress Turner. But it was too late to take it back.

"Maybe. I'll think about it," Turner said. "After what happened in Valdosta, I'll have to lay low for a while."

Gino felt relieved that Turner wasn't interested and quickly changed the subject. "What happened in Valdosta?"

"You don't wanna know what happened in Valdosta, kid," Turner said. "So, don't ask again."

"Alright, sure."

"What I need right now is a place to stay. You got a place, don't ya?"

"A small one, yeah."

"Good. I'll stay with you, then."

Gino shrugged and took a bite of his burger. This was all too sudden. It had come out of nowhere and it left him off balance. He regretted ever writing Turner and letting him know where he lived. Turner was in prison then, and Gino didn't think about him getting out on parole so soon.

But now here he was and there was no getting rid of him.

Chapter 6

The women's room at the bus station was filthy and smelly and only had cold water. The girl washed her face and hands with a cake of soap from her canvas bag and used her own towel to dry off with. Picking up her bag, she went into a stall and changed into a simple faded pink dress with spaghetti straps. She replaced the work shoes with sandals then put her work clothes back in the bag with the towel and soap.

Walking out of the restroom, she found an abandoned newspaper on a bench. She took it over to the light above a map of the town on one wall and slowly began turning its pages. When she came to the help wanted section, she stopped and began going through the listings. In a while something caught her attention. She tore out a small section and oriented it with the map, making a mental note of the physical location of the address in the ad.

Putting the newspaper back on the bench, she folded the torn out section and put it in her dress pocket. Then, picking up her bag, she walked to the front of the station into the fog. It was like a living virus, creeping and crawling over the landscape and sucking the color from everything it touched.

The girl took three steps and gave a start as something bumped hard against her leg. Instinctively she reached back for the barrette but stopped when the eerie silence of the night was broken by a loud meow. Reaching down into the swirling mist, she came up with a black-as-coal, green eyed cat. She held it purring in her arms.

"I guess you're the welcoming committee, huh Mr. Cat?" the girl said.

She walked away into the fog with her bag over one shoulder and the cat in her arms. Its body felt soft and warm. She remembered reading somewhere that a cat's temperature was much higher than a human's. Holding it gently, she petted it as she walked along. It rubbed its cool nose against her neck and sang.

Leaving the bus station behind, the girl walked up the street. "It said 21 Pine Street," she said to the cat. It meowed in reply.

After several twists and turns, she came upon a street sign and looked up into the lamp light to read it.

"Nope," she said to the cat, "but it's close."

Fifteen minutes later she was facing a white, two story house. It was dark inside. She walked quietly across the lawn and along the narrow alleyway between the tall wooden privacy fence and the building. Making her way cautiously past the garbage cans and around to the rear of the house she stopped and smiled at what she saw.

There was barely any fog back there because the fence blocked it out. She noticed the small swimming pool with its concrete sidewalk and the narrow lawn that ran around it. Next to the pool was a standing hammock and near that was a bench.

The girl put the cat down by the hammock, un-slung the canvas bag from her shoulder and undressed. She quietly slipped into the pool, swam around for a few minutes, then came out. Getting the towel from her bag, she dried herself off, put her dress back on and laid on the hammock. The cat jumped up and snuggled close to her.

The girl was very tired and didn't want to sleep but knew she would because she was exhausted. Sleep meant dreaming of shapeless things chasing her and smothering her.

After the dream, she would wake up crying and think of her husband and the child she had lost.

The overcast sky was beginning to clear. There was a half-moon above, reflecting in the waters of the pool. She stared at it. It looked very friendly. Suddenly everything looked and felt friendly. The cat, the pool, the hammock, even the house seemed friendly.

It was as if she was in a sanctuary, a place where she was meant to be. For the first time since traveling all those long miles, she felt as if her long, perilous journey was over. She was in a calm, safe harbor at last.

Smiling, she stroked the cat. It nudged her neck and purred happily. Soon they were both asleep. The girl didn't have any bad dreams that night.

Chapter 7

Gemma was almost asleep on the chaise lounge when she thought she heard noises out by the pool. She quickly blamed it on her imagination and soon drifted off.

Lately, she took to hearing sounds in her mind that weren't real. Often, out of the corner of her eye, she thought she saw shadowy shapes moving about, but there was never anything there. In addition to that, her short term memory was pretty much gone, as well.

The truth be told, she had resigned herself to her condition a long time ago. It was all part of growing old and being alone. She thought she would probably stay alone until the day she died. She was fine with that. Chalk it up to her being a cranky and stubborn old cracker.

As she awoke in the morning, Gemma picked up the book she had been reading from the floor. She placed it on the end table next to the chaise lounge, turned off the table lamp and yawned. She was about to go into the kitchen, it was just off the lanai, when she saw someone come up to the lanai door. At first, she was startled, then puzzled, then curious. Through the glass louvers it appeared to be a young girl in a worn, pink dress carrying a canvas bag slung over her shoulder.

After knocking once, the girl opened the door, stepped into the lanai and looked around. When she saw Gemma, she stared at her in surprise. Gemma stared back, thinking it took some gall for this girl to just walk in like that and stare at her, especially without permission.

The girl smiled and said very softly and sweetly, with a Hispanic accent, "Am I am too early, senora? If so, please forgive me, and I shall come back later."

"Too early for what?" Gemma asked harshly.

"Work, senora," the girl answered.

"Work? What work? There isn't any work."

The girl took a piece of newspaper from the pocket of her faded dress, unfolded it, and held it up.

"It says here that you want someone to clean around your house, senora. And to sleep in, too?"

"Oh, that? That add is over two weeks old. Anyway, it also says to phone first, doesn't it?"

"Ah, I don't have a phone, senora."

"And it also says to bring references, doesn't it?"

"References?" The girl looked puzzled. "I don't know what that is, senora."

"You don't seem to know much of anything, do you, girl?"

"Ah, no, senora, I guess I don't."

"You guess you don't, huh?" There was an uneasy moment of silence as Gemma studied the girl. "You're one of those bean pickers, aren't you?"

"Yes, senora, I am a bean picker."

"And the season is over now, isn't it?"

"Yes, senora, it is over."

Gemma sighed heavily. "For heaven's sake, girl, you waltz in here looking like a fugitive from a hurricane with no references and dressed in a faded rag and you think I'd hire you? You must be crazy as a loon!"

The girl looked hurt and Gemma suddenly felt she had gone too far and said too much. She was getting old and mean. She had forgotten how it was to be young. She had never been as poor as this girl was, or as far away from home.

She saw that the girl was clean and her hair was fixed neatly in a bun behind her neck, secured with a metal barrette. In a decent dress, she could be taken for someone's maid.

"Well, at least you've got manners," Gemma said. She smiled and chuckled. "Some of those others that came for the job really got my goat. One was real snippety. And all the other one wanted to do was sleep and eat. Ha! She couldn't clean anything if her life depended on it. So, I got rid of her real quick."

"Yes senora."

"So, you're looking for something temporary, until the picking starts again, are you?"

"Si, senora."

"Don't call me senora. I don't like that. I'd rather be called ma'am. Can you say, yes, ma'am?"

"Yes, ma'am. If you want me to."

"Well, maybe I do," Gemma said. She liked to feel in control. "Stand still!"

Gemma stepped closer to the girl and walked around her, checking her out, thinking what to do about her, considering the possibilities.

She was tall and strong. The canvas bag she carried looked like it had seen its last days and it probably held all her earthly possessions. The threadbare pink dress she wore had been washed so many times you could almost see right through it. For a girl, she had big feet more suited for farming than wearing fancy shoes.

Yet, she was very pretty and stood proud. Gemma liked that. Also, this girl looked strong, and Gemma liked that too because it balanced out her own frailness.

But there was only one problem, this girl was an illegal, most likely from Mexico. They were all over the place these days, everywhere. But it didn't seem to matter to the farmers. They hired them, worked them to the bone and got rid of them. There was no obligation to make their lives any better. They had no rights, they were expendable.

And now, here was one asking Gemma for a job. The old lady asked herself what should she do? She searched her mind for a self-serving answer. She could hire this girl temporarily and if it didn't work out she could get rid of her easily enough. It might be interesting to hear about this girl's life. It would be nice to have someone to talk. When she got tired of her, she could send her back to the fields and forget she had ever existed.

But, there was a deeper reason to have someone around. Gemma was beginning to feel the dull ache of loneliness. Being alone in a big house wasn't as bearable as it once was. It was beginning to press down on her. Once a week conversations with the pool boy weren't enough anymore.

"Well, sorry to have bothered you ma'am," the girl said, and started to leave.

"Now wait a minute, girl," Gemma said, trying to sound practical. "Hold on a minute. Maybe we can figure something out." The girl turned to face her. "Maybe we could try something on a temporary basis. A try out, maybe."

"Oh, sure, a try out," the girl said. "Si, yes."

"Maybe just a week or two first," Gemma said. "And if that works out, well, we'll see how it goes. Is that okay with you?"

"Oh, sure, ma'am!" The girl's face lit up and she smiled happily and her eyes sparkled.

"That's better than nothing, right?"

"Yes, ma'am, it is." The girl sounded more than grateful.

"What's your name?" Gemma asked.

The girl hesitated a moment, then said, "Rosarita, Rosie." Gemma thought it was a lie but let it pass. She didn't much care to know the girl's real name. She had no intention of getting that close to her. No, best to keep an emotional distance between the two of them.

"Well, Rosie," Gemma said, "my name is Mrs. Duvalier. You can call me that, or ma'am, whichever you like."

"Could I call you Mrs. Dee, ma'am?"

Gemma gave that some thought. "Alright, if you want to." Gemma liked the sound of Mrs. Dee. She smiled and said, "Can you cook, Rosie?"

"Oh, sure, Mrs. Dee. I am a pretty good cook."

"And I guess you're pretty hungry, too?"

"Oh, yes, Mrs. Dee," the girl said. "I am very hungry!"

"Good, because I'd like to have breakfast now, Rosie," Gemma said. "So, let's go into the kitchen and see what we can find to eat."

The young girl, who called herself Rosie, followed the older woman into the kitchen thinking, *"What luck! This will be like a beautiful vacation!"*

All the while, the cat was purring in its asleep out by the pool on the hammock.

Chapter 8

Structure. As far as Gemma Duvalier was concerned, life was all about structure. It was the only thing that made sense and kept her sane.

They ate a hearty breakfast and put the kitchen back in order. Rosie picked up her canvas bag and Gemma took her upstairs to see the bedrooms. There were three of them and they went into the master bedroom first. It had a big, four poster bed, a chest of drawers, and a walk-in closet. It also had its own bathroom. The window overlooked the back yard and the pool. It was open and a breeze stirred the lace curtains and draw-shade.

"This is where I sleep," Gemma said. "Do you have a bathing suit?"

"No, ma'am."

"Well, I have some from when I was young. They might still be good if the moths haven't gotten into them."

She went to the chest of drawers by one wall and began opening and closing them and moving things around. Finally, she stopped, took up a thinking pose for a moment, then chuckled.

"In there," Gemma said. She went into the walk-in closet and turned on the light. Rosie followed her in. "I forgot, they're in here."

There was a larger chest of drawers in the closet. On top of it was a single barrel shotgun. The old lady ignored it as she pulled open the top drawer, then the middle drawer.

Rosie's eyes were fixed on the shotgun. "Is that your gun, ma'am?"

Gemma ignored the gun. "Oh, no. That was my husband's. He loved to hunt."

"Do you hunt, too, ma'am?"

"Well, I did hunt a little. He taught me how to shoot and all. I was good, too. But when it came to skinning skunks, I drew the line." There was a pause and then, "Here they are!"

Gemma took several vintage, one piece bathing suits from the drawer and set them on top of the chest. She held a blue one up in front of Rosie and made a judgment as to fit.

"It might be a tad tight, but it should work. I don't use the pool anymore, but you can." She handed it to Rosie and put the rest away. "Come on, I'll show you where you'll be sleeping."

They walked across the hall into one of the smaller bedrooms. Its window looked out on the front lawn and street. Besides a single bed, it had a small bathroom with a stand-up shower. It was also furnished with a chest of drawers, and an armoire, but no walk-in closet.

"You can sleep here," Gemma said.

"Oh, it is very nice, ma'am," Rosie said. She chuckled thinking she had never slept in such a bed or had such a place with a bathroom such as this. Perhaps it was all a cruel joke and any moment now she would be told to leave or the police would come. "Thank you, ma'am." It was that politeness again. It went straight to Gemma's heart.

"You're very welcome, Rosie. Very welcome."

Rosie left her bag and the bathing suit there and they went downstairs to the lanai. Sitting on folding chairs they faced each other at the card table, near the wall.

"Alright," Gemma said with authority. "This is how it will be. I like things to be structured. It's important to structure things in life. It gives you a feeling of security and well-being. Don't you agree?"

"Oh, yes ma'am," the girl said, even though she had no idea what structure meant.

"In the mornings, we'll eat breakfast and then we'll clean house. There's a lot of cleaning that needs to be done. The windows need washing and the curtains need to be changed. Both bedroom floors have to be mopped, waxed, and polished."

The old lady went on with a long list of things that had to be done. The oven in the kitchen stove was filthy, the rug in the lanai needed to be vacuumed, the alleyway had to be swept and hosed down, and the pool deck needed washing down, too, and the louvre windows in the lanai needed dusting.

When she was finished with the list, Gemma added, "But we only clean in the morning, after breakfast. At one in the afternoon we have a light lunch and at two we listen to the radio, to the soap operas for an hour because I don't want to miss anything there. After that you're free until six because I'll be taking a nap. At six, you'll make the evening meal. Again, something light. After the evening meal, I usually like to read. Do you read, Rosie?"

"No, ma'am, I don't read very much."

"I like to read. I read the Bible quite often. Especially the Old Testament, the Psalms." Gemma paused, looking thoughtful for a moment. "Do you believe in God, Rosie? I'm sure you do."

Rosie thought about what had happened to her husband and baby. She shrugged and replied, "I try to believe in God, Mrs. Dee."

"Oh, you mustn't lose faith, Rosie. God sends his angels down to help and guide us. We should be grateful for that."

"I suppose so, ma'am."

"I'll read that Psalm to you, someday. The one about angels. Would you like that?"

"Oh, sure, I would like that. It's very nice of you ma'am, thank you."

"You're perfectly welcome," Gemma said, thinking things were off to a good start.

Suddenly the girl said, "Ah, forgive me for mentioning it, ma'am, but..." she stopped there, waiting for permission to continue.

"Yes?"

"Would I get any money?" The girl suddenly knew she had said the wrong thing.

Gemma's eyes narrowed and her lips pursed a bit. She suddenly didn't look very happy. "Pay? Ah, well, I was thinking more along the line of room and board, in exchange for work. Don't you think that would be fair? However, if you don't..."

Gemma left the last words unsaid, but clearly inferred. It was either take it or leave it.

"No, no, you are right. I shouldn't have asked. I am sorry for asking, ma'am."

Again, Gemma was caught off guard by that unexpected politeness. The girl looked genuinely sorry. Gemma saw this and said. "No, you were right to ask." She paused for a moment to consider the request. "You know, it just occurred to me that an allowance might be in order. Yes, maybe five dollars a week."

Without hesitation, Rosie accepted the offer, afraid Gemma might change her mind. "Oh, yes, ma'am. That would be very good of you. Thank you so much!"

The girl reached across the card table and took one of Gemma's frail hands in her big bear paws and pressed it. The old lady suddenly realized it was the first flesh-on-flesh human contact she'd had in many years, and it was very nice. She felt the strength in the girl's big, calloused hands.

The girl thought to herself, *"On the outside she tries to be hard, but inside she is soft. Maybe we will like each other."*

Chapter 9

Once a day, Rosie would go out to the pool to look for the cat. Sometimes it was not there and she wondered why. Finally, she figured the cat was most likely staying at the bus station in town, where she found it. That's probably where someone had abandoned it in the first place, so it thought the bus station was its home.

One Friday afternoon, while Gemma was taking her nap, Rosie took a broom and dustpan out to sweep the pool deck. She had just finished when the cat came leaping over the fence. It rubbed against her leg once, purred, and then jumped up on the hammock. Rosie went over and stared down at it.

"Well, mister cat, where have you been? I thought you and I were going steady." The cat blinked its eyes and stretched. "Okay, if that's how you feel about it. I'll just go look for a new lover, then."

"Will I do?" a voice behind her said.

She turned and saw the pool boy coming out of the alley towards her. He went over to the pump, set his gear down and stood staring boldly in her direction. She stared back. They both felt a moment of discovery and were pleased.

To Gino, it felt like being in a crowd and seeing a fascinating face. He dared not turn away for fear it would disappear. He had the feeling that if he blinked it would be gone in an instant and he would never see it again.

Suddenly, there was a loud noise out in the road and the feeling faded as quickly as it came.

"You're the pool boy. Mrs. Dee told me about you," Rosie said.

"Yeah, well she never told me about you," Gino replied in an off handed manner. "Who are you anyway?"

"I work for her."

"Since when?"

"A few days ago."

Gino sneered and chuckled. "Where did you get that dress, at a hurricane sale?"

From the look on the girl's face, Gino realized he had hurt her. He didn't know what to do to fix it. Rosie put the broom down and walked quickly past him into the lanai. She looked as if she was about to explode. Gemma, who was laying on the chaise reading, sat up and took notice.

"What's the matter, Rosie? You look upset."

"That pool boy. I don't like him, Mrs. Dee."

"Oh? Did he do something?"

"He didn't do anything," Rosie said, "but he has a big mouth."

"Oh, dear," Gemma said. "Well, just stay here until he's finished. Then he can't bother you."

Rosie nodded and replied sullenly, "Alright."

Suddenly they heard a cat's hissing and bawling, and the pool boy yelled out in pain and swore.

"Is that a cat out there, Rosie?" Gemma asked, bewildered.

"Ah, I guess so, ma'am."

Gemma got up and walked over to the window and looked out through the louvres.

"But we don't have a cat, do we, Rosie?"

"No ma'am," Rosie said quickly, "but I saw one out there yesterday taking a siesta. Maybe it lives someplace around here." A little lie wouldn't hurt.

Gino walked into the lanai holding his left hand. It was scratched but not bleeding. "That cat scratched me, Mrs. Duvalier, look!"

"Who told you to touch it, pool boy?" Rosie smirked.

"You shut up, bean picker!" Gino said, trying to sound offended.

"Now calm down, Gino," Gemma said. "I'll get the first aid kit." She went off into the kitchen.

As Gino went over to the card table to sit down, Rosie chuckled. "What a phony."

"Hey, I'm hurt here, girlie! This ain't funny!" Gino said, sneering at Rosie, "You're nothing but a bean picker, so what do you know?"

Gemma came back with the first aid kit. She took out some iodine and band aides and starting treating the scratch.

"He ain't hurt, Mrs. Dee," Rosie taunted. "It's all an act."

"You shut your mouth, bean picker!" Gino whined unconvincingly.

Gemma let out a big sigh. "Lands sake, you two are fighting like an old married couple! If I didn't know better, I'd think you two have been married for fifty years or more!"

That outburst shut them both up until Gemma finished treating the scratch. Gino stood up and whined, "That cat, ma'am. It might have rabies. Maybe I should see a doctor."

"That cat is cleaner than you, pool boy." Rosie said.

Gemma went to the stand. Gino watched closely as she opened the top drawer and pulled out some bills and put the rest back. She came back to him and offered him the money.

"Here Gino," she said. "This is for a doctor."

"Don't you take that money," Rosie growled.

Ignoring Rosie, Gino took the money and turned to leave. At the door, he stopped, walked back and handed the money to Gemma. "No, ma'am, Mrs. Duvalier. It's just a scratch, like she said. Thank you anyway."

Gino went out to finish working on the pool. The two women stared through the louver windows, looking for the cat. It was gone, so they watched Gino.

"He's such a nice boy," Gemma said.

"He's pretty," Rosie said. Gemma laughed.

As Gino was finishing up, Rosie went back out to continue sweeping the pool deck. He picked up his gear and stood watching her.

"I'm sorry for giving you a hard time," he said. She ignored him. He had that little boy lost look on his face. Finally, he shrugged. "Well, see you around."

"Yeah, sure, okay," Rosie said, as Gino left.

Rosie chuckled. She thought, *I got you but good, pool boy.*

As she stood there listening, she heard his truck start up and drive away. She had a feeling that he was interested in her, and wanted to see her again. She would have to be careful. There was no way that she would be able to fit into his life or him into hers. There was just no way.

Chapter 10

For some reason, Turner took a keen interest in Gino's work. One time he even made the arounds with him. He sat in the truck, studying the houses while Gino went in to clean the customer's pools. Then he asked questions about the customer, personal questions like who lived there and when did they go on vacation, questions like that.

Turner noticed Gino spent more time at one house than any of the others. He wondered why. "Who lives there?" Turner asked casually, as they drove away.

"Nobody, just some old lady."

"Does she live all alone?"

"She did, but now she's got a Mexican chick staying with her," Gino said with a smirk.

"An illegal, huh?"

"Yeah. One of those bean pickers."

"How old is the old lady?"

"Gosh, I don't know, really old."

"Some of those old bags have a pile of greenbacks stashed away in a mattress. You hear about it all the time."

"Not this one."

"How would you know?" Turner said. "She might. I bet I could find out real fast."

"You're not thinking of making a hit on her, are you?" Gino asked. He sounded concerned.

"Maybe."

"She's just an old lady, Turner. She ain't go no money hidden in no mattress, man!"

Turner took out his switchblade, opened it and started cleaning his fingernails. He stared down at his fingers as he talked. "You know, kid, in prison you were a pretty good boxer but you had one big flaw."

"Yeah? What's that?"

"You would never finish the other guy off. You always went for the decision. You played it safe. I'd scream at you, 'Kill the bum! Murder the punk!' But no, you always held back and coasted to an easy decision."

Gino looked sullen. "Yeah, well that's how I am, I guess. I don't wanna hurt nobody any more than I have to. It ain't my style."

"And that's your flaw, kid, because someday somebody is gonna finish you off and never think twice."

"Is that what you think?"

"That's what I know!"

When they arrived at Gino's apartment, they walked up two flights to his small flat and went in. Getting beers from the refrigerator, they sat at the kitchen table, sipping and chewing on some stale potato chips.

"What's the girl look like? Is she a looker?" Turner asked. Gino shrugged and looked away, as if he didn't care to talk about it. Turner persisted. "Most of them are real lookers. In prison, they'd come to visit their husbands or brothers. Some of them were pretty hot!" He took another sip of beer. "Is she hot?"

"I never see her," Gino said convincingly. "When I'm out at the pool, she's busy in the house. She just got here about a week ago, so I don't know her."

Turner mulled it over in his mind. "You know, it's kind of strange, an old lady with an illegal alien." He nodded and said, "I see an angle there. Immigration violations, if she's stupid enough to swallow it."

"It wouldn't work. She'd call the cops. Then where would you be?"

"See? There you go again, thinking negative, kid. You gotta stop that!"

Turner reached across the kitchen table and patted Gino hard on the cheek several times. It hurt, and the pool boy slapped his hand away. Before he realized it, Turner had the knife against his throat. For a moment, they glared hatefully into each other's eyes.

"Go ahead," Gino said. "But you better kill me, Turner, because I'll bust you up good!"

Turner knew he had gone too far. He smiled then chuckled and put the knife away.

"Hey! It's okay! We're pals, ain't we?" Turner sat back in his chair and looked serious. "You're not forgetting how I saved you from those bad guys up in Longview when you were doing three years for petty robbery, are you, kid?

Remember how I sliced and diced that ape Branson when he tried to make you his girlfriend? You ain't forgot that already, have you, kid?"

"I coulda handled him. I didn't need any help."

"It didn't look that way to me, kid. He and his pals had you marked for marriage, pretty boy. It was me who scared them off. But I guess you forgot about that. Me and my buddy, Mankin. Remember Mankin?"

Gino nodded. "Sure, I remember Mankin. He's as crazy as a loon and twice as ugly. He has a face only a mother could love."

"Mankin was okay. More than okay. He was my back-up. Strong as an ox."

"Yeah, and as dumb as they come. He believed every word you told him."

Turner chuckled. "Yeah, he is kind of stupid, ain't he?" They both laughed. The tension died down.

"But about the old lady," Turner said. "I wasn't thinking of hurting her. I just wanna see if she's loaded or not. Heck, if she's loaded, she won't mind sharing a little. She can't take it with her when she pops off, can she? Huh? The state will most likely get it all."

"Yeah, I suppose so."

"The truth is kid, I'm about broke, see? I was planning to go down to the Keys and maybe get on a boat to the Virgins or some other island." He stopped to take another sip of beer. "I can't stay here very long. The fuzz will be hot on my tail soon."

The thought of getting Turner out of his life appealed to Gino. He suddenly didn't like him anymore and the sooner he left, the better. In prison, they'd had a different relationship. He needed Turner there, but now, here on the outside, he didn't. He was only in the way.

"So," Turner continued, "you gonna help me out on this one, or not?"

"Sure, okay," Gino said.

Turner patted him on the shoulder and smiled. "That's a good boy."

Later, when he was alone, Gino began to worry about Gemma and the girl. Something had happened between him and her. Something special. He felt it and he knew she did, too.

Chapter 11

Rosie worked hard and Gemma was glad to have her around. She especially enjoyed watching her and the pool boy do their hate-love dance. It was a dance that only the young had the strength and endurance to do. It was a chase me until I catch you, kind of thing. She had never done it herself, but had watched others do it when she was young.

But for now, Gemma's life was just as she wanted it to be. The girl was a godsend in many ways, and Gemma's earlier ultimatum of Rosie being temporary was put on hold. It was as if the girl had been her servant and companion for years. There was no reason to send her way just yet.

As for structure, now that the major cleaning was done, it didn't seem all that important anymore. Gemma was content to let Rosie work on her own while she read a book or dabbed away at her painting in the corner of the lanai. They each had their own routine now.

But one day a snake entered paradise. Rosie was out by the pool reading a magazine and Gemma was at the easel working on her painting. There was a loud knock at the front door. Gemma put down her brush and went to answer it. A man stood in the doorway staring at her. He was paunchy and wore a seedy looking, much worn suit and had his hat pulled down low on his forehead.

"Ah, ma'am..." the man started to say. Gemma cut him off.

"No thank you, sir. We don't need any. Perhaps you should try next door."

The man chuckled. "Oh no, lady, I ain't selling nothing. I'm from Immigrations."

Gemma gave a start. Her heart beat rapidly and her mind raced. Finally, she found the right words. "Can I see some identification, sir?"

The man didn't answer very quickly He looked away for a moment then back at her. "Ah, I left it in my briefcase, lady."

"In your briefcase?"

"Yeah, out in the car?"

"Where's the car, sir?" Gemma asked, looking up and down the street.

"Around the corner."

It was a rapid fire back and forth exchange and it quickly left Gemma full of doubt as to who this man really was. First of all, he had the smell of beer on his breath and secondly, his suit and shoes looked awfully worn and untidy, as did his hat.

"Wait here and I'll call my husband," Gemma said. She started to close the door, but couldn't because the man had his foot pressed against it.

"I think you ain't got no husband, lady," the man said.

He pushed his way into the hallway and grabbed Gemma's wrist. She gasped in pain.

"You're hurting me, sir!" Gemma strained to pull away. The man released his grip and she rubbed her wrist. He took a switchblade knife from his pocket and opened it.

"Please don't hurt me!" Gemma cowered against the wall.

The man shut the door. "Let's go into the lanai," he said.

He pushed Gemma ahead of him. She went quickly through the hallway to the rear of the house with him close behind. When they got to the lanai, he glanced around for a moment then walked up to the louvre windows and looked out. He stared intensely for a moment, then turned back to Gemma.

"Do you know her?" Gemma asked.

"Be quiet!" the man said.

"You're not from immigrations, are you?"

The man said, "Nope!"

"Well, what do you want?"

"Spending money."

"I don't keep much money in the house, sir."

"Sure you do," the man said. "Over in that." He nodded at the stand.

Gemma's eyes suddenly narrowed. This man knew a lot about her. Too much for a stranger. She went to the stand and opened the top drawer. "How much spending money do you want, sir?" Her voice trembled.

"I want whatever's in there and hurry it up."

Gemma took out a pile of bills. Her hands shook so badly she dropped some. She bent down to get them, but had trouble getting back up.

"Make it snappy," the man growled. He waited a moment, glancing nervously out at the pool. Then, suddenly exasperated, he said, "Damn if you ain't a slowpoke, old lady!"

He grabbed the money out of her hands and shoved her aside. She backed into the easel and the painting crashed loudly to the floor. Gemma struggled to stay on her feet. She leered angrily at the man.

"Who sent you?" she asked.

"I told you to be quiet!" the man muttered as he fumbled clumsily in the drawer for more money. He dropped some bills and bent down to pick them up. As he did, he heard someone coming into the lanai. Knowing it was the girl, he dropped the money, got up, and turned to face her with the switchblade held out.

Rosie came in close and the man made a lunge to cut her. She quickly danced to the left and brought her right hand back to her hair. As the knife narrowly missed Rosie's neck, she swung the cat's claw across his line of vision.

Turner felt a burning sensation on his right cheek. It quickly became a burning pain. Blood ran down the side his face. Uttering a groan, he put a hand to the injured spot, backed away, and glared hatefully at Rosie. Cursing her, he ran from the lanai.

Rosie had started after him, but stopped. "Let him go," Gemma said in a raspy voice.

"Are you alright, Mrs. Dee?" Rosie asked, turning to her.

"Yes, I'm alright," Gemma said. She went to the card table, sat down and stared blankly at the floor. Fear was in her eyes. She looked about to cry. "Did he cut you?" she asked Rosie.

"No, I'm okay." Rosie began picking the money up from the floor.

"He said he was from immigrations. I knew that was a lie right away. He stared at you, out at the pool. Have you seen him before? Do you know him?"

"Me? Seen him before?" Rosie looked away before answering. "No, ma'am, I never saw that gringo before." She knew he was the man on the bus from Valdosta.

"Well, he kept staring out the window at you, so I thought...well, never mind. After what you did to him, I'm sure he won't be coming back here again.

Rosie only shrugged. "Maybe." She handed the money to Gemma. She put it back in the stand while Rosie picked up the painting and set it back on the easel.

"Strange, though," Gemma said, "he seemed to know about the money and where it was."

Rosie nodded. "Yeah, that is strange." She paused, then said, "You know, Mrs. Dee, he might come back."

Gemma's face tightened and her eyes narrowed.

"Well, if he does, I'll be ready for him. He'll be sorry he ever messed with this old lady!" Then she said, "What did you hit him with, Rosie? By the way he ran out of here, you must have hurt him pretty badly."

"It was this," Rosie said, taking the barrette from her dress pocket. She walked closer to Gemma and held it out for her to see. Gemma stared at it for a moment.

"Is it a weapon? It looks like it is."

"Yes. Someone gave it to me."

Gemma pointed at it and said, "There's some blood on it. Better wash it off."

Rosie took it into the kitchen. After washing and drying it she put it back in her hair and went back to the lanai.

"Suddenly I'm hungry," Gemma said, "Let's go make cucumber sandwiches and later I'll read from the Psalms."

As Gemma and Rosie stood in the kitchen making sandwiches, Turner went running up the street holding his bloody cheek. Gino was waiting for him up ahead, in his truck, as planned.

"What the hell happened?" Gino asked as Turner jumped into the cab. He saw that something had gone terribly wrong and Turner had promised him nothing would.

"She cut me, is what happened!"

"Who, the old lady?"

"No, the girl!" Turner said with a groan. "I've seen her before. She's the one I saw on the bus from Valdosta!" He groaned again. "Give me something, quick!"

Gino got a paper towel from the glove compartment. Turner took it and pressed it against his face.

"I had a handful of greenbacks when the girl came in and cut me," Turner growled. "But I'll fix her. Oh, will I ever. Wait until she meets Mankin!"

Gino gave Turner a questioning look. The one person he never wanted to see again was Mankin. Mankin was cruel, sadistic, and insane beyond belief. Mankin was the devil in the flesh.

The pool boy suddenly realized he was in way over his head. In addition to that, he had put the old lady and the girl in danger.

Chapter 12

"I still don't understand, Rosie? How did that man know so much about us? Someone must have told him about me. He seemed to think I had a lot of money. I just don't understand it at all."

"You know, Mrs. Dee, I think the pool boy had something to do with this," Rosie said.

Gemma considered that for a moment, then said, "Oh no, I don't think so, Rosie. Gino is such a nice young man. He has manners and all. No, I think you're wrong there."

"Well, I'm not so sure about that, Mrs. Dee."

"Not Gino, Rosie. No, not Gino. That boy is like a son to me. He wouldn't do me any harm."

"Yes, but maybe he has friends who aren't so nice. Do you know what I mean?"

Rather than argue her point, Rosie left it hanging. For the next few days there was no mention of the incident and life returned somewhat to normal. The encounter with Turner was pushed aside.

Late one afternoon Rosie was sitting on the bench by the pool brushing her hair. Gemma, who was in the lanai, watched her for a while and then went out and took the brush from her hand.

"Let me do it," Gemma said, and started brushing the girl's hair. She smiled at Rosie. "You've had a hard life, haven't you, Rosie?"

Rosie shrugged. "Yes, I suppose so, Mrs. Dee," she replied, sounding as if she was resigned to it.

"You can talk to me about it, if you want to," Gemma said. "I'd like to hear it."

"It is not a pretty story, Mrs. Dee. You wouldn't like it."

"Well, let me be the judge of that, Rosie," Gemma replied, putting the brush down on the bench.

Rosie shrugged. "Alright, if you want, I will tell it to you." Rosie replied, then fell silent for a moment as she thought about where to start.

She cleared her throat and began telling Gemma about how her parent's small farm in Chiapas was part of a large farm that belonged to a rich land owner. The work was hard and life was a dead end with no future. When a baby was born the mother and father prayed for a boy because a boy could take over when the father fell sick or got too old to work. Most of the old farmers died in the field with a hoe in their hands.

Girls were married off as early as age twelve. They would go live with their husband on his parent's farm. Rosie had been married off at the age of sixteen and was lucky to get a gentle, husband who respected her. Although he was not handsome, he was kind and gentle. She never fell in love with him, but she respected him because he was good to her. That was enough for Rosie.

She went on, telling Gemma how she became with child and how it all ended so tragically that awful day when the landlord's soldiers fired into the crowd of farmers killing her husband and many others.

She summed up her story by telling Gemma about her leaving the corn vender's shack and subsequently ending up at Gemma's house several years later. When she finished, she noticed that Gemma was very quiet. Her eyes were moist and on the verge of tears.

"Are you alright, Mrs. Dee" Rosie asked.

Gemma wiped her eyes. "That was very sad, Rosie."

"Yes, but that is life and you can do nothing about it."

"That's true, even when you see it coming."

"Yes and when you don't see it coming, it hits you harder."

"It happened to me once."

Rosie turned to face Gemma on the bench. "It happened to you once?"

"Oh, yes. When I was young, just like you."

"I would like to hear about that, Mrs. Dee, I really would."

Gemma smiled sadly and stared over at the house for a moment, as if it played a part in her story. "I don't know, maybe I shouldn't."

"Why not, Mrs. Dee?"

Gemma sighed and shrugged. "Well, it's a little painful, even though it happened some time ago."

"In Chiapas, we have a saying: If you tell a sad story to someone, you will feel better and the other person will feel sad. Then, for the other person to feel good again, they must tell a sad story to someone else."

Gemma chuckled. "We call that passing the buck."

"But it works, ma'am," Rosie said. "Try it, you will see."

"Alright," the old lady said, "but let me have a moment to get my thoughts together, although I really shouldn't have any trouble because it's been with me all these years. It never goes away. There are some things you never forget."

Rosie put her hair in order and put the barrette back in place. "Yes," she said. "That is true."

Gemma waited a moment, then sighed. She was ready to tell her story.

"When I was young, and an only child, Rosie, my parents drowned in a boating accident out in the Gulf. But they left me well off with plenty of money and stock investments and that sort of thing, including the house. I had grandparents then, but they're gone now too."

Gemma stopped a moment to sort out her words, then went on.

"I wasn't a pretty girl. The fact was, I was plain and shy. Boys hardly took notice of me or tried to date me. I didn't dream of marrying like the other girls did. By the time I was twenty five I had given up on that. Then, one day when I was sitting all alone in the park reading Jane Austen, it happened."

"What happened?" Rosie asked.

"He finally came and noticed me.

"He?"

"Yes, Robert Sherwood. He came and noticed me."

"Who was Robert Sherwood?"

"Robert Sherwood went to the same high school as I did. He was the school hero, the star quarterback on the football team, the boy most likely to succeed. Robert was so handsome that the girls screamed and fainted if he so much as looked at them. And he dated them all, at one time or another. He was every girl's dream."

"Gosh!" Rosie whispered.

"After graduation Robert sort of drifted out of sight. Rumors had it that he was selling aluminum siding in Tampa. Or maybe it was encyclopedias, I forget what exactly. I even heard he was in Africa, leading safaris out into the bush and that he had been killed by a lion, or crushed by an elephant or something. I knew that he liked to hunt a lot. He was a member of the local hunting club and loved guns."

"So, you two got together?"

"Yes. This very handsome man just swept me off my feet one day in the park, while I was all alone reading Jane Austen. I fell completely and helplessly in love with him. And what woman wouldn't have? He was dashing and bold, and had a silver tongue and a way with words. I soon became the envy of every girl in town. For the first time in my life I felt beautiful and important. So, when Robert asked me to marry him, I didn't hesitate to agree."

"Were you happy?"

"Oh, yes. Very happy. We took our honeymoon in Spain and sailed around the world. It was a storybook marriage, for a while."

"Only for a while? What happened?"

Gemma rubbed her palms together, shrugged and looked away for a moment.

"What happened? Like I said, Robert Sherwood happened, Rosie." Gemma spoke in a flat, cold tone, her eyes narrowing. "When we finally settled down here, in the house, things began to change. I began to see little chinks in Prince Charming's armor. I soon realized that Robert had no intention of going to work. He was as lazy as a cat in summer and was very content to live on my money."

"Really? He was so lazy?"

"Yes, with his slick ways and good looks, he would have made the perfect gigolo. But in addition to his laziness were his bad manners and the fact that he tried to control me and my money. To make life even more unbearable, most of the time he was pickled."

"Pickled?" Rosie asked. She looked confused.

"Yes. Pickled. Soused! Drunk! Drunk as a skunk!" Gemma said sourly. "He drank all the time, mostly whiskey. Sometimes it was hard to tell if he was drunk or sober. And when he got drunk he became base and vile and mean. Really mean, if you know what I'm saying?"

"He hurt you, Mrs. Dee? Is that what you're saying?"

"Yes. That's why I had the miscarriage, a baby girl, Sylvia." Gemma's voice drifted off, sounding far away, fading out. She looked down at her hands again.

"How horrible," Rosie said. She stared at Gemma a moment and asked softly, "And after that?"

"After that, things got worse," Gemma replied. "Robert took a mistress, a young girl from town." She nodded her head. "Oh, everybody knew what was going on. They had a good time laughing at me. I became the town fool, the clown."

"What a *postizo*! What a rat!" Rosie said. "I would have cut his *cahones* off!"

Gemma chuckled. "He needed something cut off, alright."

"If I was here at the time, I would have done that for you, Mrs. Dee. With pleasure, believe me!"

"Thank you, Rosie," Gemma said. She smiled affectionately at the girl.

"Go on, Mrs. Dee, finish your story, please."

Gemma nodded and continued. "Well, I never felt good after the miscarriage. In my mind, I mean. I had bad dreams and nightmares and I felt deeply depressed all the time. A month after I got out of the hospital, it was October then, Robert told me that he was going to have a Halloween party out by the pool. There would be decorations and catered food and music. All his friends would be there."

"Was that to cheer you up?"

Gemma chuckled sarcastically and stared past Rosie as if seeing a vision. "That's what I thought at first but when his mistress showed up, I knew different."

"He brought her here, his mistress, to your house?"

"Oh, indeed he did, Rosie, right under my nose. They danced around the pool under a Halloween moon and kissed like two lovers. It's strange how I remember that moon. It had this sort of pale, orange glow to it. It looked so big. In the old days, they used to call a moon like that a hunter's moon."

There was a moment of quiet as Gemma's face took on a tortured look. It seemed as if she was lost in thought, visualizing an agonizing scene from the past.

"What did you do then, ma'am?" Rosie asked. Gemma seemed not to hear her. "What did you do then?" she repeated.

Gemma suddenly gave a start as if coming out of a trance. She shuddered and folded her arms across her stomach and looked past Rosie with a distant, blank stare.

"What did you say, Rosie?"

"What did you do then, Mrs. Dee?"

"What did I do then?" Gemma's voice sounded strange. She paused for a second, then said angrily, "Well, I'll tell you what I did! I went upstairs to the bedroom and laid down on the bed and cried. My heart was broken and I cried and cried until my tears burned dry and I couldn't cry anymore."

"What did you do then?"

"I went to the window, looked down at the pool and screamed. I screamed as hard as I could, but no one paid any attention to me, what with all that music and laugher going on. It was as if I wasn't even there, like I didn't exist. In my own house!" Gemma paused to draw in a deep breath and exhale. "In my own house!" Her voice was a loud, painful howl.

She looked into Rosie's eyes and calmly said, "And that's when I did it, Rosie."

"You, you did what?" Rosie asked with concern.

"That's when I went into the walk-in closet and got the shotgun."

"The one I saw? With one barrel?"

"No. There was another one. It had two barrels and it was always kept loaded in case somebody broke into the house to rob us. Robert had shown me how to use it. So, I grabbed it and rushed downstairs."

Rosie groaned, as if in pain and said with alarm, "Oh, no, you didn't!"

"Oh, yes," Gemma said, her voice breaking into a pitiful, whining sob. "I went down there to the pool and went walking toward Robert and the girl. When the band saw me, they stopped playing. Everyone stared at me with terrified looks on their faces, knowing what was about to happen. Robert sort of smirked at me and said something. I don't remember what he said, but he made a move to hit me or grab the gun. I don't know which."

Gemma stopped and Rosie stared at her with eyes wide, not knowing what to say, just waiting for the next words to hit her like the blows off a hammer.

Gemma started to sob and shake. "I didn't mean to hurt her." Tears were running down her face. "But somehow she got in the way when I fired the first shot. I didn't even know the poor thing's name."

"Madre de Dios!"

"I know I shouldn't have," Gemma whined in a hysterical, high pitched voice, "but when I saw Robert wasn't hurt at all, I got very angry and pulled the second trigger, hitting him. The girl fell on the deck and Robert fell into the pool. I looked down at him and could see the water turning black like oil, in the moonlight. Tiny little diamonds danced all around his body and he wasn't moving."

"You killed them both?"

"Not her. She was wounded but didn't die, but Robert did." Gemma took out her handkerchief with trembling hands. Her body shook as she went on sobbing, moving back and forth and back and forth, holding her arms across her stomach, clutching herself as if she was in pain.

Rosie reached over and held her frail body in her arms, trying to calm her. Gemma rested her head on the girl's shoulder and they sat still and quiet. No one spoke for a long time. They listened to the singing of evening birds somewhere in the distance. The sun was low in the sky.

"The police? They must have come for you," Rosie said.

Gemma pulled away and wiped her eyes. "Oh, indeed they did. There was a big trial in Tampa. I guess I had a good lawyer or maybe the jury felt sorry for me. I was sentenced to ten years in prison, but got out in seven. They were the longest years of my life."

Rosie stared at Gemma in awe, feeling a new respect for her. Gemma was no longer the spoiled old lady Rosie had first thought her to be. No, Gemma had suffered in life just as she had. There was a strong bond between them now.

Gemma put her handkerchief away and stood up. She forced a smile and looked down at Rosie.

"I feel better, now," she said. "Let's have lunch and later I'll read to you from the Psalms."

"Alright, Mrs. Dee."

Chapter 13

It was late afternoon and Rosie was sweeping the pool deck when Gino came through the alleyway. He stopped a moment to watch her.

"You still here?" Gino asked. Rosie ignored him and kept on sweeping. "I figured you'd be out picking beans again, wetback."

The derogatory word was no more out of his mouth than Rosie slapped him. The blow was so hard his knees almost buckled. He stood dazed for a moment, shaking the stars out of his head. There was a look of surprise on his face.

"Don't call me wetback, pool boy!"

"Ouch! Okay! Sorry!" Gino rubbed his cheek. His confident, arrogant smirk disappeared.

He walked over to the pump and shut it down. Taking the lid off the automatic dispenser, he began filling it with chlorine tablets. Rosie finished sweeping the deck then walked over to Gino and stood leering at him. He stopped working and got up to face her.

"What's wrong?" the pool boy asked. He looked into her eyes.

"You know what's wrong!"

Gino shifted nervously on his feet. "No I don't."

"Who is that guy?" Rosie asked.

"I don't know who you're talking about."

"You're a liar. After all she has done for you and you treat her like that? It's not right."

Gino let out a big sigh and glared at Rosie. "Look, I told you, I don't know what you're talking about, bean picker. So, leave me alone. I got work to do here!"

"He pulled a knife on her and twisted her arm Do you think that was nice?"

Gino went back to work, finishing quickly. Rosie watched him go into the lanai. Moments later, she heard him and Gemma talking. He said very little. Moments later, he came out with his head down. Ignoring Rosie, he got his gear and left.

Out on the street, Gino slammed the pool gear down into the back of the pickup, jumped in and drove quickly across town. Ten minutes later he jammed on the brakes, leaped from the struck and charged blindly up the stairs into his apartment.

"Turner!" he yelled as he burst in.

What he saw waiting there made him come to a sudden stop. His blood turned cold and a look of fear came over his face.

A man called Mankin stood next to the kitchen table while Turner sat in a chair smiling. The table was stacked with empty beer bottles and a half full bag of potato chips.

"Hi, kid," Mankin said. "The boys in the cellblock told me to say hello. They miss you!" Mankin tried to laugh but his voice sounded more a dog's bark.

He stood almost seven feet tall, had big arms and broad shoulders. His face was weathered, wrinkled, tanned, and scarred. It was a face that had been punched, kicked, smashed, and cut. It had a pushed in nose, deep set eyes under a bulldog's forehead, and a wide sneer that revealed rotting and missing teeth. His fists were like huge sledge hammers.

"When did you get out?" Gino asked, trying to sound casual.

"I didn't. I'm still in!" Mankin laughed hard at his own joke, then took a swig of beer.

Gino walked slowly to the refrigerator and got a bottle of beer. He sat down at the table across from Turner who had a bandage on the right side of his face where Rosie had cut him.

Gino stared at him, his mind racing. This was bad. Very, very bad. He knew that Mankin had probably busted out of prison and stole a car, which was what he was good at. And here he was, right smack in the center of Gino's kitchen.

The pool boy's thoughts were interrupted when Turner reached for the bag of potato chips and knocked it over. Chips spilled out onto the table.

"You're a real slob, Turner, you know that?"

"You're a real slob, Turner, you know that?" Turner said, repeating the young man's words in a mocking tone.

"Go to hell," Gino said.

Turner uncoiled like a snake. In a second he had one hand around Gino's throat and a knife blade pointed at

Gino's face. The young man slowly placed his beer on the table and went stiff and quiet.

"Shut it!" Turner sneered. "You're like that bitch up in Valdosta. I had to close her yap for good! I left little pieces of her all over Georgia!"

Turner shoved Gino hard, sending him tumbling backwards off his chair. He ended up flat against the wall in a sitting position, clutching his throat and coughing.

"Why did you hurt the old lady? You didn't have to hurt her," Gino cried in a hoarse voice.

"Yeah? Well, you can blame it on that bean picker," Turner said. "Everything was going as planned until she jumped in. I had the money right here in my hand. A thousand bucks! A thousand bucks!" The veins on Turner's forehead stood out.

"Well, you'll have to leave, Turner," Gino said. He got up off the kitchen floor. "You can't stay here anymore."

Turner chuckled. "Oh, we're leaving alright, kid. Right after I get the money from that crazy, old dame." He sneered and nodded. "Only this time it ain't gonna be them two against me. Mankin is gonna take care of the girl, right, old buddy?"

Mankin nodded and smiled. "Yeah. I'm gonna peel her like a banana, kid! Me and her is gonna have a party! Oh, yeah!"

Suddenly Gino launched himself headfirst at Mankin. Swinging hard, he tagged the giant with a vicious right to his jaw. The big man shook the blow off and grabbed a fistful of Gino's shirt. Holding the pool boy at arm's length, Mankin clubbed him in the face. The young man collapsed in the giant's arms, half unconscious.

"Bring him over here," Turner said, setting the chair upright by the table. Mankin slammed Gino hard onto it. The pool boy moaned in pain. There was a deep, bloody cut above his left eye and his nose was broken.

"Don't do this, Turner!" Geno whined in a whisper. He could barely talk. His nostrils were clotted shut so he had to breathe through his mouth. He glared pleadingly at Turner.

"Nothing personal, kid, but you're a loser. You always were."

"Don't go over there Turner, please! I'll get the money for you, I swear I will!"

"I guess the bean picker got to you kid. How sweet," Turner said with a chuckle. "True love, huh?"

Mankin said, "I'll be getting a piece of yer girlfriend in a little while, kid. Too bad you won't be there to see it."

"If you touch her I'll kill you!" Gino groaned. The effort to talk hurt. His head hung slack to one side. "I swear I will!"

Mankin looked at Turner. "Maybe I should finish the punk off, huh, you think so?"

Turner sneered at Gino. "Sure, go ahead." Then he quickly reversed himself. "Maybe not."

"Why not? He's askin' for it."

"It's best to keep things simple. We get the money and head west. Maybe Vegas."

"How much you think she's got stashed away?"

"Could be ten, twenty, even fifty grand," Turner said. "Old broads like her usually keep it stashed under a mattress in the bedroom."

"Supposin' she's got it hid and won't tell? Then what?"

"Then I'll introduce her to my friend here, Mr. Switchblade."

"Don't do it, Turner!" Gino yelled, groaning from the effort. "Please! I'm begging you. Don't!"

"Put his lights out," Turner told Mankin. "His blubbering is making me sick."

"My pleasure," The big man answered with a sadistic chuckle. He walked over and slammed his fist against Gino's jaw, snapping his head sideways. The pool boy groaned and his body went slack.

"Nice shot," Turner said. "Let's have a beer." He reached into the refrigerator for two beers and handed one to Mankin. They drank it quickly and left.

It was almost dark when they went out to Mankin's car. Fog was beginning to form in the streets and the air was turning cooler. Driving slowly across town, they parked near Gemma's house. As they sat in the car talking, the fog got denser and higher. They never noticed it. Their minds were on the old woman and the girl.

"Remember what I told you," Turner said. "Don't let the girl get her hand back in her hair. She's got something sharp there. That's how she cut me."

"Don't worry about it. I'll tear her arm right off, if she makes a move." Then, "Is she a looker? You said she was a looker."

"Yeah, she's a looker alright. She turned the kid's head real fast," Turner said. He lit a cigarette and took a few puffs and then put it out in the ash tray. "Come on pal, let's go get the money."

"Yeah," Mankin replied anxiously.

As they got out of the car, they quickly became aware of the deep darkness. Chest high fog roiled like live tentacles all around them. No one, not a single soul, was out and the sidewalks and streets were hidden in a damp, undulating, strange mist. It was thick as soup on the lawns which made the houses hard to see. The fog pushed the light back into windows. It was difficult walking because there were hardly any street lights here in this old part of town.

They took a few steps and became disoriented. It was difficult to tell up from down or left from right. Turner stumbled when the sidewalk ended at a crossroad. Moments later, Mankin tripped and disappeared under a shroud of gray fog. A cat shrieked out in pain.

Turner heard him groan. "Mankin! What happened?"

"A cat!" Mankin gasped painfully. "It tripped me!" The big man big man rose out of the fog and struggled to get back on his feet.

"You okay?" Turner asked. He looked around, as if he was lost.

"I twisted my ankle. It might be sprained! Maybe worse!" Mankin sucked in air and moaned in pain.

They walked a few more steps and Turner called a halt. "What's the matter?" Mankin asked.

"I'm not sure where we are. This fog has screwed me up."

"Are you serious?" Mankin sighed, shook his head and swore.

Turner said, "Wait here. I'll look and see if we passed her place."

Without waiting for a reply, Turner disappeared into the fog. Mankin shifted his weight to his one good ankle and lit a cigarette. He groaned in pain and swore again.

Chapter 14

Gemma sat across from Rosie at the card table and read to her from Jane Austen's, *Northanger Abbey*. She finished the last words of the fifth chapter, closed the book and smiled.

"There. We'll stop here. It's time for tea and sandwiches," Gemma said.

"Huh? Oh, sure, Mrs. Dee." Somewhere, not far away, a cat let out a piercing, painful yowl.

For a second, Rosie gave a start then froze. She pushed her chair back from the table and stood up slowly. Approaching the lanai door, she opened it and stared into the night. Fingers of fog drifted in on the cool air. She listened for a moment then quickly closed and locked it. She stared at Gemma.

"Mrs. Dee, we have to hide!"

"What?" Gemma asked. She could see the concern on Rosie's face.

"We have to hide!"

"Hide? What for?"

"They're coming to kill us."

Rosie grabbed Gemma's arm. The book went flying from her hand as the girl pulled her towards the kitchen. "Where can we hide, Mrs. Dee? We gotta hide quick!"

"Have you gone crazy?"

Suddenly the lanai door burst open. Mankin and Turner rushed in, bringing swirls of fog with them. Mankin was holding a snub-nose revolver, and Turner had his switchblade knife out.

A cat yowled mournfully outside by the pool. Gemma and Rosie stood motionless in front of the kitchen door, uncertain of what to do.

Rosie started to reach back for the barrette. Mankin saw her and moved fast. He lunged at her and struck her hard on the jaw with his huge fist. The barrette went flying across the room. Rosie's head spun sideways and her legs buckled. As she started to fall, Mankin caught her by the arm with his free hand and held her up.

"Good move, pal," Turner said. He waved his knife. "Take her out to the pool. There's a bench out there. Have some fun. I'll handle this end."

"A bench?" The giant chuckled as he stared lasciviously at Rosie. She made a feeble effort to get loose, but couldn't break his grip. "Let's go have a bench party, baby."

"Please, don't hurt her, sir!" Gemma yelled. "Please!"

Mankin ignored the old woman. He dragged Rosie outside into the dark, limping and grimacing in pain at each step. Turner saw the barrette where it lay on the floor, He walked over, stared at it for a moment and chuckled.

"So, this is what she cut me with?" he said, picking the barrette up "Well, after my pal finishes with her, it'll be my turn. Then we'll see how she likes it." He put the barrette in his jacket pocket.

"Why are you here? What do you want, sir?" Gemma asked in a firm voice.

"Don't play dumb with me, old lady," Turner growled. "You know what I want."

"Money?"

"Yeah, money. You ain't got nothing else that interests me," Turner said.

He went to the stand and pulled open the top drawer. Glancing in for a moment, he started grabbing bills and stuffing them into his coat pocket. When he was finished, he turned to look at the painting on the easel and smirked. "Not bad, but I wouldn't buy it." He laughed at his own joke.

"You have the money, now please go, sir!" Gemma said. "Please go!"

Turner walked over to Gemma, grabbed her arm and put the tip of the knife blade to her cheek. "Where's the rest, Grandma?" he hissed through yellow, decaying teeth.

"You have it all. There isn't any more."

"I'll ask again, where's the rest?"

"Please believe me, sir, there isn't any more."

Turner gave the point of the blade a little flicking motion, making a small cut on Gemma's cheek. A drop of blood appeared.

"Oh!" Gemma gasped in pain.

"I'll ask one more time, then I'll cut you good. Where's the rest of the money?"

"Alright! It's upstairs!" Gemma whined loudly, on the verge of crying. Her body shook violently.

Turner sneered. "See how easy that was?" he said. "Wasn't that easy?"

"Yes," Gemma said, nodding.

"Okay, then, let's go get it!"

Turner gave her a hard shove. Gemma staggered backwards until she regained her balance then turned and walked unsteadily into the hallway. She gripped the stairway bannister with trembling hands and made her way to the upper landing. Once there, she went into the master bedroom, turned on the light and stood staring at Tuner.

"Stay here," he said and walked quickly over to the opened window to stare down at the pool area. He listened for a moment then yelled down, "You okay, pal?"

Mankin had just laid Rosie's half conscious body cross the bench by the pool. He turned and squinted up at the yellow shaft of light in the bedroom window.

"Yeah, man, I'm doing great. Gonna have a party! Oh, yeah! Ride 'em cowboy! Yippy-khi-yai-aay!"

Mankin shifted the revolver to his left hand. Reaching down with his right one, he tapped Rosie on the cheek. "Hey, wake up, little darlin'! It ain't no fun if you're gonna sleep on me."

Rosie shook her head to clear it. She raised halfway up on the bench. Leering at Mankin, she groaned, "Who the hell are you, *gringo*?"

"Me? Why, I'm yer lover boy, little darlin'! Lover boy! Haw!" Mankin chuckled as he shoved her back down on the bench.

Rosie drove her right foot up into the big man's groin as hard as she could. Mankin groaned in pain and staggered backward on his injured ankle. The snub-nose revolver went off with a loud bang just as a figure come leaping out of the fog. It landed on Mankin's back and got a strangle hold around his neck. The giant tried to shake it off as he hobbled about in a circle, grunting and groaning.

Rosie realized the attacker was Gino, and he wasn't doing very well. Mankin had gotten a hand back into Gino's hair and was pulling hard. Gino howled in pain. As Rosie got up, she felt a dull pain and a hot wetness in her right side. Ignoring it, she jumped in, grabbing one of Mankin's legs.

All three collapsed on the pool deck with Mankin's head slamming against the concrete with a skull cracking sound. He moaned once and went quiet. Gino kept a chokehold on him, digging his thumbs into the giant's windpipe with all the force he could muster. He kept the pressure on until he was satisfied Menken wasn't breathing any more then sat back panting for air.

Up in the master bedroom, Turner snickered and said, "Sounds like they're having fun down there." He turned his attention to Gemma. "Okay, let's get this over with. Give me the rest of the cash."

"Will you leave then, sir?"

"Sure. Why would I stay here?"

"Alright. I believe you," Gemma said, going to the walk-in closet. "It's in here, I'll get it for you."

Before Turner could answer, Gemma opened the door and went in. He was about to follow her when he noticed that everything had suddenly gone quiet down by the pool. He paused for a moment, went to the window and looked out.

"Hey, Manken! Having fun?" There was no answer. "Don't hog it all! Save some for me, pal!" He listened for a second. It was strangely quiet down below. "Mankin, are you okay?"

"Mankin's taking a nap, Turner!" Gino yelled back.

Turner stiffened. "Is that you kid?"

"Yeah, it's me."

"I should have finished you off, kid!" Turner growled. "Yeah, I should have put you away for good."

"I'm coming up to get you, Turner!" Gino yelled.

"I wouldn't do that, kid," Turner said. "I got the old lady here. You come up and I'll cut her in pieces. You know what I can do with a knife."

"Okay, okay," Gino said quickly. "I'll stay here."

"Good. As soon as I get the money, I'll come down and take care of you and the wetback! So, just you sit tight."

Turner's words had no sooner left his mouth than Gino and Rosie heard a shotgun blast. Turner's body came flying through the open window. It spiraled downward and landed in front of the lanai with a sickening thud. Rosie and Gino stared at each other, stunned. Gino walked to Turner's body where it lay in the light shining from the lanai windows.

"Don't come over here," he told Rosie. "He's looks like fresh hamburger."

"Dead?"

"Oh, yeah, really dead."

After a pause, Rosie said, "She used that shotgun she had in the closet. You should go up and check on her, see if she's alright. I'll be up in a minute." She spoke in a whisper.

"Are you alright?" Gino asked.

"Yes. Go to her."

Gino turned away from the body and rushed through the lanai up to the bedroom. He found Gemma sitting on the bed sobbing, the shotgun clutched tightly in both hands. He went to her, gently took the weapon, placed it on the floor and sat down beside her.

"We'll have to call the police," Gino said, "but she can't be here when they come."

"Why not?"

"Because she's an illegal." Gino said.

"But, where can she go?"

"On my boat, for a few days, until it's over."

"What should we tell the police?"

"We'll say I was having dinner with you when these guys busted in to rob you. They're were both on the run and wanted for murder, so that should help us."

"Yes," Gemma replied. "I'll tell them I shot the short one. His pockets are full of my money. You can shoot intruders in your house, if they threaten you. It's the law, I think," Gemma said righteously. "Anyway, I already have a record of shooting people with a shotgun." It almost sounded funny.

"It should work," Gino said. "I'll say the big one took me out by the pool to kill me but I got the best of him."

Suddenly Gemma said, "Where is she, Gino?"

Gino stood up. "Downstairs. She said she was coming. I'll go check."

"I'll go with you," Gemma said. They both left the bedroom and walked down the stairs to the lanai. Rosie wasn't there so they went out to the pool to look around in the dark. When she saw Turner's body, she shivered and quickly looked away.

"Rosie!" Gemma whispered loudly. "Where are you, child? Are you alright?"

Gino walked past Mankin's body to the bench. Noticing something glistening, he put his hand down to feel what it was. A large amount of half dried blood had puddled there.

"She's hurt!" he said loudly.

In a panic, he ran out to the front of the house and stood looking around. Gemma came hurrying alongside of him. When they didn't see her, Gemma whined, "Dear God! Oh, Gino, please go find her! Bring her back!"

"Alright. She can't be far."

Gino got in his truck and drove slowly down the street looking left and right. The fog had thinned down a little, making it easier to see. A cool breeze was blowing it away.

Soon, he heard a continuous, loud meowing. He slowed down, looking from side-to-side through the truck window, trying to figure out where it came from. Suddenly, on the driver's side, he saw something on the sidewalk. A big, black cat stood next to a figure down on its knees, holding its side.

Slamming on the brakes, Gino leaped from the truck, ran to Rosie and held her in his arms.

"You darn fool! You trying to die on me?"

"What do you care, pool boy."

"I care, I care," Gino sobbed. "I care!" He began to cry.

Picking her up in his arms, he gently placed her in the truck, then got in next to her. She looked pale in the moonlight. Her breathing came slow and shallow.

"Take me home, pool boy," she whispered. "Take me home to my *casita* in Chiapas."

"Alright," Gino replied. Tears streamed down his face. He wiped his eyes and started driving east out of town. Rosie laid her head on his shoulder.

"Do you love me, pool boy?"

"Yes, I loved you from that first day I saw you."

"I knew it." Rosie smiled, then sighed

They didn't talk any more. A few miles east of Hudson it was all farmland, green and sweet smelling. Rows of variegated vegetables stretched to the horizon. The scent of growing things lay heavy in the air.

Rosie turned her head to stare from the truck window. The sun was just coming up over the fields, yellow, bright and pure. Rosie nodded, slowly raised a hand and pointed to the field.

"Chiapas," She said softly. "Chiapas."

Gino stopped the truck, got out and ran to the edge of the field. He picked up a small clod of soft, moist soil and quickly brought it back to Rosie. Placing it gently in her hand, he helped her raised it up to her face for a moment so she could inhale the salty-sweet, earthy scent.

She smiled at Gino and said, "I'm home..."

* * *

It was midafternoon when Gemma Duvalier walked along in front of a row of headstones in a little cemetery in the town of Hudson. She held a small bouquet of mixed flowers in one hand. In the other she carried a book. On her head was a wide brimmed hat, worn to keep the sun off her silver hued hair.

She stopped by a bench near the far end of the row and turned to face a large headstone. It was a fine, well carved, ornate, expensive looking headstone. The name below the carved angel at the top, read: "Rosie Duvalier." It had the usual information about the place and date of birth, and date of death, except that the date of birth was missing. Below this were the words, "Gemma's Angel." Below that was a short quote from the Bible that said something about the Lord sending angels to earth to help people through their trials and tribulations.

Gemma placed the flowers at the foot of the headstone and sat down on the bench. She opened the book and began to read aloud, as if reading to someone. As she sat there reading and losing track of time, the shadows grew longer and the sun became a soft, orange glow on the horizon. Darkness was not far off.

A black cat came out of somewhere and rubbed against Gemma's leg. She put the book aside, reached down, picked the cat up, and petted it for a while. Finally, she put the cat down, picked up the book, and walked away. The cat stared after her for a moment then turned to squint and blink at the gravestone. It purred as it laid its sleek body down and curled up on the flowers.

The End

About the Author

R. Annan is a seasoned and traveled author with many interests. As a career serviceman, he served in Korea and Vietnam. He also completed a one-year course at the Defense Language Institute at Monterey, California, and graduated from the University of South Florida with a B.A. in Art and Art History. After taking a two-year course in screenwriting at the Hollywood Scriptwriting Institute, he established The Old Time Radio Club Time Machine as both a scriptwriter and an actor.

Other books by R. Annan: *Mr. Dobbs: A Christmas Ghost Story*; *The Ghost of Reginald Burton, Esquire*; *Vzor's Prisoner: A Sci-fi Novel*; *The Princess of Ovaar: A Sci-fi Fantasy*; *Sen Loi*.

Western novels by R. Annan include: *The Fight for the Lazy M*; *The Red Bandana*; *The Salvation of Trace Logan*; *The Cowboy from Sierra Blanca*; *Jack Cordell Westerns*; *Clay Jared Westerns*; *Jesse Garnett Westerns*.